P's and Q's
WERE NEVER THIS FUN!

Bored with board games? Had it with meaningless computer scenarios? Need a new challenge for car trips, rainy days, work breaks, whatever? Try the puzzlers that don't require even a pencil—just the power of your brain . . .

☞ THE NUMBERS GAME ☜

Answers to the puzzles on the back cover:

- 40 days and nights of the Great Flood
- 1 wheel on a unicycle
- 90 degrees in a right angle
- 32 degrees Farenheit at which water freezes
- 64 squares on a checkerboard

THE NUMBERS GAME

by

GRAHAM PERRY

WARNER BOOKS

A Time Warner Company

WARNER BOOKS EDITION

Copyright © 1993 by Graham Perry

Cover design and illustration by Jerry Pfeiffer

Warner Books, Inc.
1271 Avenue of the Americas
New York, NY 10020

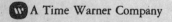 A Time Warner Company

Printed in the United States of America

First Printing: June, 1993

10 9 8 7 6 5 4 3 2 1

CONTENTS

THE NUMBERS GAME
Introduction

Okay. Figure this out:

$$24 = \text{h. in a d.}$$

It might look like the kind of algebraic equation you sweated over back in high school. But it doesn't take a genius to realize the answer is "hours in a day."

That's how simple it is to play *The Numbers Game*. Just plug in the words that match the number. So easy a child could do it.

Ah-hah, but it gets trickier. As you move through this book, you'll find some number puzzles that aren't quite as simple as the time of day. To solve all of the puzzles requires a little knowledge of everything—from sports to geography to the opera—and some imagination.

So if you've worn out Trivial Pursuit; if the Sunday crossword puzzle has you boggled, and Boggle requires a few friends—try *The Numbers Game*.

Oh, and just in case you get stuck, there is a "help" section of clues preceding our answers, which are in the back of the book. Please note that these are *our* answers, and others are possible. Have fun!

THE NUMBERS GAME

9 = p. in the s. s.

_____ ✍

9 = i. in a b. g.

_____ ✍

10 = f. in b.

_____ ✍

4 = q. in a f. g.

_____ ✍

3 = p. in a h. g.

_____ ☞

100 = y. in a f. f.

_____ ☞

206 = b. in the h. b.

_____ ☞

3 = b. in "L. of the R."

_____ ☞

3 = w. in "M."

_____ ✍

66 = b. in the K. J. B.

_____ ✍

10 = a. in the B. of R.

_____ ✍

26 = a. to the C.

_____ ✍

11 = f. in a c.

_____ ✍

80 = c. in a m.

_____ ✍

1760 = y. in a m.

_____ ✍

5280 = f. in a m.

_____ ✍

18 = i. in a c.

_____ ✍

"50 = W. to L. Y. L."

_____ ✍

4 = w. on a c.

_____ ✍

1 = K. K. on the E. S. B.

_____ ✍

5 = m. b. in "J. and the B."

———————————————————— ✍

52 = p. c. in a d.

———————————————————— ✍

100 = y. in a c.

———————————————————— ✍

10 = y. in a d.

———————————————————— ✍

30 = d. in J.

_____ ✍

5 = p. in a n.

_____ ✍

2 = n. in a d.

_____ ✍

2 = q. in a h.-d.

_____ ✍

9 = l. of a c.

_____ ✍

5 = G. L.

_____ ✍

15 = m. of f. per p., a. to A. W.

_____ ✍

57 = v. of H.

_____ ✍

4 = s. in a d. of c.

_____ ✍

2 = t. in the W. T. C.

_____ ✍

64 = y. o. w. I. h. y. w. s. n. m.

_____ ✍

2 = w. s. in "C."

_____ ✍

3 = p. in a b. s.

_____ ✍

1000 = y. in a m.

_____ ✍

7 = s. of S. the S.

_____ ✍

1 = t. o. k.

_____ ✍

"3 = m. and a b."

_____ ✍

4 = i in M.

_____ ✍

4 = s in M.

_____ ✍

2 = p. in a b.

_____ ✍

1 = w. on a u.

_____ ☞

3 = w. on a t.

_____ ☞

3 = W. M. at B.

_____ ☞

6 = A. of A.

_____ ☞

49 = r. a. in a r.

_____ ✍

1 = s. s.

_____ ✍

99 = b. of b. on the w.

_____ ✍

28 = d. in F.

_____ ✍

29 = d. in F. in a l. y.

_____ ✍

6 = w. in the U.S. S.

_____ ✍

12 = u. in a d.

_____ ✍

50 = s. on the A. f.

_____ ✍

13 = s. on the A. f.

_____ ☞

24 = s. z. of i. t.

_____ ☞

6 = h. d. of o. for R. C.

_____ ☞

93,000,000 = m. in an a. u.

_____ ☞

200 = m. in a c.

_____ ✍

3 = f. in a y.

_____ ✍

10 = p. in C.

_____ ✍

50 = s. in the u.

_____ ✍

1 = the l. n.

_____ ✍

2 = c. b. as b. as o.

_____ ✍

3 = b. in the h. e.

_____ ✍

12 = d. of C.

_____ ✍

46 = c. in a h. c.

_____ ✍

1000 = w. in a k.

_____ ✍

60 = s. in a m.

_____ ✍

12 = A. at the L. S.

_____ ✍

13 = o. c.

_____ ✍

24 = h. in a d.

_____ ✍

10 = C. g. to M.

_____ ✍

7 = p. of E.

_____ ✍

7 = h. of R.

_____ ☚

7 = d. in "S. W."

_____ ☚

6 = w. of H. VIII

_____ ☚

2 = w. that d. m. a r.

_____ ☚

8 = K. H. of E.

_____ ✍

26 = l. of the R. a.

_____ ✍

4 = s. of the y.

_____ ✍

12 = m. of the y.

_____ ✍

3 = s. to the w.

_____ ✍

2 = s. of a l. t.

_____ ✍

80 = d. to g. a. the w.

_____ ✍

365 = d. in a y.

_____ ✍

3 or 4 = "B. K."

_____ 🖎

12 = t. of I.

_____ 🖎

366 = d. in a l. y.

_____ 🖎

40 = d. in L.

_____ 🖎

2 = R. in the W. H.

_____ ✍

"3 = M."

_____ ✍

7 = a. of m.

_____ ✍

"7 = P. of W."

_____ ✍

5 = b. in the T.

_____ ☜

1000 = s. l. by the f. of H. of T.

_____ ☜

15 = m. on the d. m. c.

_____ ☜

2 = c. in the t. by C. D.

_____ ☜

18 = h. on a g. c.

_____ ☞

8 = S. r.

_____ ☞

3 = O. K. C. f.

_____ ☞

"500 = H. of B. C."

_____ ☞

24 = b. b. in a p.

_____ ✍

87 = f. s. and s. y.

_____ ✍

30 = d. h. S.

_____ ✍

3 = b. in "G."

_____ ✍

3 = s. and y. o.

_____ ☞

4 = b. in a w.

_____ ☞

1000 = p. of l.

_____ ☞

1001 = "A. N."

_____ ☞

14 = l. in a s.

_____ ✍

9 = s. by B.

_____ ✍

4 = l. in a d. w.

_____ ✍

3 = o. a m.

_____ ✍

4 = m. in a s.

_____ ✍

6 = "B. C."

_____ ✍

3 = r. in a c.

_____ ✍

5 = m. in C. R.

_____ ✍

4 = c. in the h. h.

_____ ✍

4 = i. in a s. q.

_____ ✍

4 = s. in a b. q.

_____ ✍

"101 = D."

_____ ✍

8 = c. in a m.

_____ ✍

8 = d. in H.

_____ ✍

2 = p. in a p.

_____ ✍

2 = w. w.

_____ ✍

7 = d. s.

_____ ✍

4 = U.S. p. on M. R.

_____ ✍

212 = d. F. at w. b. p.

_____ ✍

4 = o. in "The R. of N."

_____ ✍

32 = d. F. at w. f. p.

_____ ☞

4 = H. of the A.

_____ ☞

18 = v. a. in the U. S.

_____ ☞

"12 = C." of a. R.

_____ ☞

116 = y. in the H. Y. W.

_____ ✍

4 = t. FDR e. p.

_____ ✍

7 = w. of the a. w.

_____ ✍

2 = E. of E.

_____ ✍

$4 = $ g. in C.

_____ ✍

$6 = $ d. in the S.-D. W.

_____ ✍

$1 = $ i. by l.

_____ ✍

$2 = $ i. by s.

_____ ✍

11 = s. in the C.

_____ ✍

755 = h. r. h. by H. A.

_____ ✍

9 = j. on the U.S. S. C.

_____ ✍

14 = p. in W. p.

_____ ✍

3 = b. of the U.S. g.

_____ ✍

2 = h. of C.

_____ ✍

100 = c. in a d.

_____ ✍

435 = s. in the H. of R.

_____ ✍

5 = s. in a p.

_____ ✍

3 = s. in C. f. v.

_____ ✍

2 = P. J. P.

_____ ✍

6 = d. of c.

_____ ✍

95 = M. L. T.

_____ ✍

40 = y. in the d. for the I.

_____ ✍

2 = t. the p. a. r.

_____ ✍

500 = F. c.

_____ ✍

"3 = F. of E."

_____ ☞

"12 = A. M."

_____ ☞

90 = d. in a r. a.

_____ ☞

360 = d. in a c.

_____ ☞

"1 = D. in the L. of I. D."

_____ ✍

106 = e. in the p. t.

_____ ✍

7926 = m. in the e. d.

_____ ✍

9 = m. in a h. b. g. p.

_____ ✍

5 = v. o. in the h. b.

_____ ✍

4 = q. in a g.

_____ ✍

2 = p. in a q.

_____ ✍

12 = d. in a g.

_____ ✍

2 = w. in a f.

_____ ☜

4 = y. in an O.

_____ ☜

150 = P. in the B.

_____ ☜

12 = l. of H.

_____ ☜

3 = l. p.

_____ ✍

3 = b. m.

_____ ✍

4 = m. of the B.

_____ ✍

13 = a b. d.

_____ ✍

9 = G. M.

_____ ✍

"3 = S." in C. p.

_____ ✍

2 = B. G.

_____ ✍

3 = s. in a t.

_____ ✍

4 = s. in a s.

_____

4 = s. in a r.

_____

3 = p. of an i.

_____

8 = l. on a s.

_____

6 = s. in a h.

_____ ✍

8 = s. in an o.

_____ ✍

1 = e. on a C.

_____ ✍

16 = o. of m.

_____ ✍

12 = s. of the z.

_____ ✍

"100 = Y. of S."

_____ ✍

"20,000 = L. U. the S."

_____ ✍

2 = l. in the h. b.

_____ ✍

"3 = C. in the F."

_____ ✍

4 = e. of the p. u.

_____ ✍

4 = U.S. s. with the w. *N.*

_____ ✍

2 = H. of P. in E.

_____ ✍

3 = t.v. m. about A. F.

_____ ☞

3 = d. for J. in the b. of the w.

_____ ☞

40 = d. in the w. for J. C.

_____ ☞

1440 = m. in a d.

_____ ☞

3 = p. c.

_____ ✍

7 = c. in the r.

_____ ✍

5 = f. on a h.

_____ ✍

5 = t. on a f.

_____ ✍

2 = w. on the W. H.

_____ ✍

3 = l. on a t.

_____ ✍

61 = h. r. h. by R. M. in o. s.

_____ ✍

10 = f. in h. of a b. r.

_____ ✍

24 = d. p. to the I. for M. I.

_____ ☜

2 = e. k. of a. on N. A.

_____ ☜

200 = d. for p. "G." in M.

_____ ☜

6 = p. in a p. t.

_____ ☜

4 = g. to w. the W. S.

_____ ☞

2 = o. in a d. p.

_____ ☞

48 = m. in a p. b. g.

_____ ☞

102 = f. in the E. S. B.

_____ ☞

22 = J. H. "C."

_____ ✍

"7 = B. for S. B."

_____ ✍

"10 = D. that S. the W."

_____ ✍

"9 = S." by J. D. S.

_____ ✍

9 = c. of h. in the "D. C."

_____ ✍

226 = p. in this b.

_____ ✍

HELP

If you're really stumped,
but you don't want to check the answers yet,
here are some additional clues to the puzzles.
We didn't want to make it too easy,
but these should be all the help you need.

PAGE 3

- approach system-atically
- games people play
- it's up your alley
- no two-minute warning needed

PAGE 4

- this one is rink-y dink
- don't fumble this one
- one is connected to the next one
- can be Hobbit-forming

PAGE 5

- toil and trouble
- lots of chapter and verse
- feel free to speak
- it's your right to add more

PAGE 6

- weights and measures
- a miss is as good as a . . .
- ditto
- ditto

PAGE 7

- weights and measures
- this is simple, Simon
- sometimes they all drive
- 'twas beauty killed the beast

PAGE 8

- you need to stalk this one
- four suits, too
- twentieth going on twenty-first
- as time goes by

PAGE 9

- one is for dad
- sometimes they come from heaven
- it's small change
- ditto

PAGE 10

- some have nine tails
- a Superior collection
- just ask Famous Amos
- are you playing catch-up?

PAGE 11

- not a two-piece or a three-piece
- now second fiddle to Sears
- and Paul M. is getting close
- don't slip-per on this one

PAGE 12

- dress for success
- can you name Han Solo's spaceship?
- anchor's aweigh
- I hear you knocking

PAGE 13

- and diapers
- muddy waters
- ditto
- unless it's underwear

PAGE 14

- take a balanced approach
- tri, tri, tri again
- follow a star
- only in New York

☞ HELP ☜

PAGE 15

- all of them good ones
- join the chorus (line)
- next verse same as the beginning
- don't leap to the conclusion

PAGE 16

- requires a leap of faith
- five of them Democrats
- unless you're a baker
- with below, they're forever

PAGE 17

- see above
- start at Greenwich
- no obligation to get this one
- an astronomical number

PAGE 18

- the kind Bugs won't eat
- but we have only two
- look to the north
- the last to join are hot and cold

PAGE 19

- song
- same song
- one is a hammer, one an anvil
- song

PAGE 20

- some of us have X, some have Y
- Watson, you get me steamed
- in the nick of time
- but one of them left

PAGE 21

- these were once revolutionary
- what a difference a —— makes
- thou shalt not get a clue
- these came before above

PAGE 22

- when here, do as they do
- you're dopey if you miss this
- the lucky ones got a divorce
- you should get this right

PAGE 23

- the last was Elizabeth's dad
- easy as a, b, c
- Vivaldi put them to music
- as the world turns

PAGE 24

- don't drink and sail
- don't take one to school
- says Verne
- plus one quarter

PAGE 25

- they're Russian
- lost in the desert
- add one every four
- starts on Wednesday,
  ends on Sunday

PAGE 26

- they were cousins
- they're better with swords
  than guns
- woman, too
- so said Lawrence

PAGE 27

- Genesis is one
- She must have been beautiful
- answer's good for a bottle of rum
- it was the best of times

PAGE 28

- even when they're miniature
- lost without the red-nose
- such a merry old soul
- another hat went on a cat

PAGE 29

- not a tasty treat in my book
- Honest, Abe said it
- nights, too
- get this one just right

PAGE 30

- at the old ball game
- same as above
- George said so
- Ali and Aladdin are here

PAGE 31

- Will S. wrote some beauties
- most like to take the Fifth
- watch your language
- don't burn your fingers

PAGE 32

- it takes a lot of notes
- play them Bach to Bach
- ask P. T. Barnum
- they start at noon, doo-dah

PAGE 33

- this should get your pulse going
- they all need tuning
- they croon next to a striped pole
- all of them spotted

PAGE 34

- every night a light
- some people spell it with a *C*
- round, green, mushy
- let's hope they will be the last

PAGE 35

- pride, sloth, and so forth
- they're set in stone
- don't get steamed over this one
- get this one before the
     fat lady sings

PAGE 36

- this one is on the rocks
- the real final days
- take a poll on this one
- one got stabbed in the back;
  another fiddled

PAGE 37

- didn't they get tired of fighting?
- and then HST
- you'll wonder about this one
- uneasy lies the crown, these days

PAGE 38

- Mrs. Mao and her pals
- in 1967
- a midnight ride
- ditto

PAGE 39

- how to secede in business
- he had a hammer
- but only one is a Chief
- he wanted to end the war
  to end all wars

PAGE 40

- can you balance your checks?
- all under one dome
- all hard-earned
- a full house

PAGE 41

- the biggest one's in Arlington
- but they never really
  reached America
- both infallible
- one more was for resting

PAGE 42

- he nailed them to a door
- Holy Moses!
- the mailman's signal
- when fortune smiles upon you

PAGE 43

- Joanne Woodward's countenances
- are they your peers?
- a matter of degree
- ditto

PAGE 44

- Russian novel
- a table with no legs
- it's not a small world
- longer for whales and elephants

PAGE 45

- you need every one of them
- milk it for all it's worth
- ditto
- that's lots of twelves

PAGE 46

- the Brits say so
- it's Greek to me
- fear no evil
- strong man's job

PAGE 47

- fat, pink, and cute
- a sad tail
- yeah, yeah, yeah
- that's one for good measure

PAGE 48

- found in muse-ums
- Russian siblings
- this is no fairy tale
- just take sides on this one

PAGE 49

- ditto
- ditto
- does this one bug you?
- keep away from water spouts

PAGE 50

- squares, add two
- an octopus can feel this one out
- this one needs 20 vision
- including us

PAGE 51

- what's yours?
- South American novel
- that's deep
- no smoking allowed

PAGE 52

- movie-title song
- let's get physical
- Mexico is one
- Lord, how Common!

PAGE 53

- we watched them all!
- the same place as Pinocchio
- what temptations!
- and you don't have one to spare

PAGE 54

- use them to make others
- Dorothy sang about it
- with nails in each one
- this little piggy . . .

PAGE 55

- but they're grounded
- take one away, it falls
- in '61
- slam dunk this one

PAGE 56

- what a bargain!
- floating zoo
- unless you go to Jail
- the music man says it's trouble

PAGE 57

- they know in Toronto
- one reason for bunting
- regulation, that is
- once it was tallest

PAGE 58

- a conundrum
- lots of couples
- catch a falling tsar
- after "The Catcher"

PAGE 59

- an Inferno place
- No way! You're on your
  own with this one.

OUR ANSWERS

PAGE 3

9 = planets in the solar system
9 = innings in a baseball game
10 = frames in bowling
4 = quarters in a football game

PAGE 4

3 = periods in a hockey game
100 = yards in a football field
206 = bones in the human body
3 = books in "Lord of the Rings"
      (J. R. R. Tolkien)

PAGE 5

3 = witches in "Macbeth"
      (William Shakespeare)
66 = books in the King James Bible
10 = amendments in the
      Bill of Rights
26 = amendments to the
      Constitution

PAGE 6

11 = fathoms in a chain
80 = chains in a mile
1760 = yards in a mile
5280 = feet in a mile

PAGE 7

18 = inches in a cubit
"50 = Ways to Leave Your Lover"
4 = wheels on a car
1 = King Kong on the
      Empire State Building

PAGE 8

5 = magic beans in
      "Jack and the Beanstalk"
52 = playing cards in a deck
100 = years in a century
10 = years in a decade

PAGE 9

30 = days in June
5 = pennies in a nickel
2 = nickels in a dime
2 = quarters in a half-dollar

PAGE 10

9 = lives of a cat
5 = Great Lakes
15 = minutes of fame per person,
       according to Andy Warhol
57 = varieties of Heinz

PAGE 11

4 = suits in a deck of cards
2 = towers in the
      World Trade Center
64 = years old when I hope you will
       still need me
2 = wicked stepsisters in
      "Cinderella"

PAGE 12

3 = pieces in a business suit
1000 = years in a millennium
7 = seas of Sinbad the Sailor
1 = time opportunity knocks

PAGE 13

"3 = men and a baby"
4 = *i*'s in Mississippi
4 = *s*'s in Mississippi
2 = pieces in a bikini

PAGE 14

1 = wheel on a unicycle
3 = wheels on a tricycle
3 = Wise Men at Bethlehem
6 = Avenue of Americas

PAGE 15

49 = reasons all in a row (Crosby,
      Still, Nash, and Young)
1 = singular sensation
99 = bottles of beer on the wall
28 = days in February

PAGE 16

29 = days in February in a leap year
6 = women in the U.S. Senate
12 = units in a dozen
50 = stars on the American flag

PAGE 17

13 = stripes on the American flag
24 = standard zones of
      international time
6 = holy days of obligation for
      Roman Catholics
93,000,000 = miles in an
      astronomical unit

PAGE 18

200 = milligrams in a carat
3 = feet in a yard
10 = provinces in Canada
50 = states in the union

PAGE 19

1 = the loneliest number
2 = can be as bad as one
3 = bones in the human ear
12 = days of Christmas

PAGE 20

46 = chromosomes in a human cell
1000 = watts in a kilowatt
60 = seconds in a minute
12 = Apostles at the Last Supper

PAGE 21

13 = original colonies
24 = hours in a day
10 = Commandments
    given to Moses
7 = plagues of Egypt

PAGE 22

7 = hills of Rome
7 = dwarfs in "Snow White"
6 = wives of Henry VIII
2 = wrongs that don't make a right

PAGE 23

8 = King Henrys of England
26 = letters in the Roman alphabet
4 = seasons of the year
12 = months of the year

PAGE 24

3 = sheets to the wind
2 = shakes of a lamb's tail
80 = days to go around the world
365 = days in a year

PAGE 25

3 or 4 = "Brothers Karamazov".
   (Fyodor Dostoyevski)
12 = tribes of Israel
366 = days in a leap year
40 = days in Lent

PAGE 26

2 = Roosevelts in the White House
"3 = Musketeers"
7 = ages of man
7 = "Pillars of Wisdom"
   (T. E. Lawrence)

PAGE 27

5 = books in the Torah
1000 = ships launched by the face
   of Helen of Troy
15 = men on the dead man's chest
2 = cities in the tale by
   Charles Dickens

PAGE 28

18 = holes on a golf course
8 = Santa's reindeer
3 = Old King Cole's fiddlers
"500 = Hats of Bartholomew
   Cubbins" (Dr. Seuss)

PAGE 29

24 = blackbirds baked in a pie
87 = four score and seven years
30 = days hath September
3 = bears in "Goldilocks"

PAGE 30

3 = strikes and you're out
4 = balls in a walk
1000 = points of light
1001 = "Arabian Nights"

PAGE 31

14 = lines in a sonnet
9 = symphonies by Beethoven
4 = letters in a dirty word
3 = on a match

PAGE 32

4 = movements in a symphony
6 = "Brandenburg Concertos"
3 = rings in a circus
5 = miles in Camptown Racetrack

PAGE 33

4 = chambers in the human heart
4 = instruments in a string quartet
4 = singers in a barbershop quartet
"101 = Dalmatians"

PAGE 34

8 = candles in a menorah
8 = days in Hanukkah
2 = peas in a pod
2 = world wars

PAGE 35

7 = deadly sins
4 = U.S. presidents on
     Mount Rushmore
212 = degrees Fahrenheit at
     water's boiling point
4 = operas in "The Ring of
     Nibelungs" (Richard Wagner)

PAGE 36

32 = degrees Fahrenheit at water's
      freezing point
4 = Horsemen of the Apocalypse
18 = voting age in the U. S.
"12 = Caesars" of ancient Rome

PAGE 37

116 = years in the
       Hundred Year's War
4 = terms FDR elected president
7 = wonders of the ancient world
2 = Elizabeths of England

PAGE 38

4 = gang in China
6 = days in the Six Day War
1 = if by land
2 = if by sea

PAGE 39

11 = states in the Confederacy
755 = home runs hit by
      Hank Aaron
9 = justices on the
    U.S. Supreme Court
14 = points in Wilson's plan

PAGE 40

3 = branches of the U.S.
    government
2 = houses of Congress
100 = cents in a dollar
435 = seats in the House of
      Representatives

PAGE 41

5 = sides in a pentagon
3 = ships in Columbus's first voyage
2 = Pope John Pauls
6 = days of creation

PAGE 42

95 = Martin Luther's Theses
40 = years in the desert for the
        Israelites
2 = times the postman always rings
500 = Fortune companies

PAGE 43

"3 = Faces of Eve"
"12 = Angry Men"
90 = degrees in a right angle
360 = degrees in a circle

PAGE 44

"1 = Day in the Life of Ivan
        Denisovitch" (Solzhenitsyn)
106 = elements in the periodic table
7926 = miles in the earth's diameter
9 = months in a human baby's
        gestation period

PAGE 45

5 = vital organs in the human body
4 = quarts in a gallon
2 = pints in a quart
12 = dozens in a gross

PAGE 46

2 = weeks in a fortnight
4 = years in an Olympiad
150 = Psalms in the Bible
12 = labors of Hercules

PAGE 47

3 = little pigs
3 = blind mice
4 = members of the Beatles
13 = a baker's dozen

PAGE 48

9 = Greek Muses
"3 = Sisters" in Chekhov's play
2 = Brothers Grimm
3 = sides in a triangle

PAGE 49

4 = sides in a square
4 = sides in a rectangle
3 = parts of an insect
8 = legs on a spider

PAGE 50

6 = sides in a hexagon
8 = sides in an octagon
1 = eye on a Cyclops
16 = orders of mammals

PAGE 51

12 = signs of the zodiac
"100 = Years of Solitude"
    (Gabriel García Márquez)
"20,000 = Leagues Under the Sea"
    (Jules Verne)
2 = lungs in the human body

PAGE 52

"3 = Coins in the Fountain"
4 = elements of the physical
    universe
4 = U.S. states with the word *New*
2 = Houses of Parliament in
    England

PAGE 53

3 = t.v. movies about Amy Fisher
3 = days for Jonah in the
        belly of the whale
40 = days in the wilderness for
        Jesus Christ
1440 = minutes in a day

PAGE 54

3 = primary colors
7 = colors in the rainbow
5 = fingers on a hand
5 = toes on a foot

PAGE 55

2 = wings on the White House
3 = legs on a tripod
61 = home runs hit by Roger Maris
        in one season
10 = feet in height of a
        basketball rim

PAGE 56

24 = dollars paid to the Indians for
      Manhattan Island

2 = each kind of animal on
    Noah's Ark

200 = dollars for passing "Go" in
      Monopoly

6 = pockets in a pool table

PAGE 57

4 = games to win the World Series

2 = outs in a double play

48 = minutes in a professional
    basketball game

102 = floors in the
      Empire State Building

PAGE 58

22 = Joseph Heller's "Catch"
"7 = Brides for Seven Brothers"
"10 = Days that Shook the World"
"9 = Stories" by J. D. Salinger

PAGE 59

9 = circles of hell in the
      "Divine Comedy"
226 = puzzles in this book